This book belongs to

....

make believe ideas

The Frog Prince

Key sound short i spellings: e, i, ui, y
Secondary sounds: fr, ss, thr

Written by Rosie Greening
Illustrated by Clare Fennell

Reading with phonics

How to use this book

The **Reading with phonics** series helps you to have fun with your child and support their learning of phonics and reading. It is aimed at children who have learned the letter sounds and are building confidence in their reading.

Each title in the series focuses on a different key sound or blend of sounds. The entertaining retelling of the story repeats this sound frequently, and the different spellings for the sound or blend of sounds are highlighted in red type. The first activity at the back of the book provides practice in reading and using words containing this sound or blend of sounds. The key sound for **The Frog Prince** is short i.

Start by reading the story to your child, asking them to join in with the refrain in bold. Next, encourage them to read the story with you. Help them decode tricky words.

Now look at the activity pages at the back of the book. These are intended for you and your child to enjoy together. Most are not activities to complete in pencil or pen, but by reading and talking or pointing.

The **Key sound** pages focus on one sound and on the various different groups of letters that produce that sound. Encourage your child to read the different letter groups and complete the activity so they become more aware of the variety of spellings there are for the same sound.

The **Letters together** pages look at three pairs or groups of letters and at the sounds they make as they work together. Help your child to read the words and trace the route on the word maps.

Rhyme is used a lot in these retellings. Whatever stage your child has reached in their learning of phonics, it is always good practice for them to listen carefully for sounds and find words that rhyme. The pages on **Rhyming words** take six words from the story and ask children to read and find other words that rhyme with them.

The **Key words** pages focus on a number of key words that occur regularly but can nonetheless be challenging. Many of these words are not sounded out following the rules of phonics, and it's best for children to learn them by sight so that they do not worry about decoding them. These pages encourage children to retell the story, practicing key words as they do so.

The **Picture dictionary** page asks children to focus closely on nine words from the story. Encourage children to look carefully at each word, cover it with their hand, write it on a separate piece of paper, and finally, check it!

Do not complete all the activities at once – doing one each time you read will ensure that your child continues to enjoy the stories and the time you are spending together. **Have fun!**

Princess Jill loved shiny things,
like twinkling jewels and crystal rings.
But Jill's most glitzy thing of all
just had to be her golden ball!

There wasn't much Jill didn't own,
but still she always felt alone.
She thought, "I'd give my things away
to have a friend for just one day."

The princess simply loves to play.
Will Jill find a friend today?

One morning Princess Jill went out
to throw her little ball about.
"I wish someone would play with me,"
the princess thought unhappily.

Jill skipped toward the river's edge,
but tripped upon a rocky ledge!
She lost her grip, and in a flash,
she dropped the ball and heard it SPLASH!

Splash!

The princess trips, to her dismay.
Will Jill find a friend today?

"My ball!" she wailed. "It's sinking down –
and if I swim, I'll wreck this gown!"
But then Jill heard a little croak.
A green-skinned frog hopped up and spoke.

8

"Excuse me, can I help at all?"
So Jill replied, "Bring back my ball!"
The croaky frog said, "If I do,
can I please come and live with you?"

The frog tells Jill the price to pay.
Will Jill find a friend today?

Jill didn't want to live with him:
he had such icky, sticky skin!
And so she thought she'd play a trick.
She said, "That's fine. Just fetch it, quick!"

"Yippee!" the frog said, diving in.
He brought the ball back with a grin.
But when Jill had her ball once more,
she sprinted home and locked the door!

The princess quickly sprints away.
Will Jill find a friend today?

The next day, Jill and old King Pip
were nibbling on some fish and chips.
They heard a little rat-tat-tat.
Pip asked his daughter, "What was that?"

Rat-tat-tat!

Someone wants to come and stay.

Will Jill find a friend today?

13

The princess opened up the door.
The frog was sitting on the floor!
His little lily pad was packed
with big, grilled flies and insect snacks.

"I'm here to live with you!" he cried.
"Oh no you're not!" mean Jill replied.
King Pip said, "Jill! That's impolite.
Of course the frog can stay the night."

The frog has packed a big buffet.
Will Jill find a friend today?

King Pip made up a little bed.
Frog had other plans instead.
He hopped upstairs in search of Jill
and napped upon her windowsill.

16

When Jill woke up, she'd had enough.
She picked the frog up in a huff.
"I think it's time you left, don't you?
This room's not big enough for two!"

She thinks the frog should go away.
Will Jill find a friend today?

The frog looked up with tearful eyes
and said, "It's really no surprise!
I'm just a silly frog, you see:
nobody will be friends with me."

The little frog was lonely too!
Jill knew exactly what to do.
"I'll be your friend," the princess said,
and quickly kissed him on the head.

18

The princess knows just what to say.
Will Jill find a friend today?

At once, the frog
began to glow . . .

his little legs
started to grow . . .

a crown appeared
upon his head . . .

. . . and soon a prince stood there instead!

A prince appears without delay.
Will Jill find a friend today?

The prince knelt down upon one knee.
"You broke the curse by kissing me!
I think I've found a friend for life –
will you agree to be my wife?"

The pretty girl said, "Yes, I will!"
The prince said, "By the way, I'm Bill."
The pair were married there, and then
and never felt alone again!

The princess married Bill that day.
She found a friend – hip, hip, hooray!

Key sound

There are several different groups of letters that make the short i sound. Practice them by looking at the words on the lily pads and using them to make sentences. Can you use each word in a different sentence?

river big

swim king little

grin kiss

pretty
English

build
quick
quit

gym   mystery
syrup   crystal
symbol

25

Letters together

Look at these groups of letters and say the sounds they make.

ss **fr** **thr**

Follow the words that contain ss to lead the frog to the princess.

ss

home

kiss

loss

door

grass

trick

princess

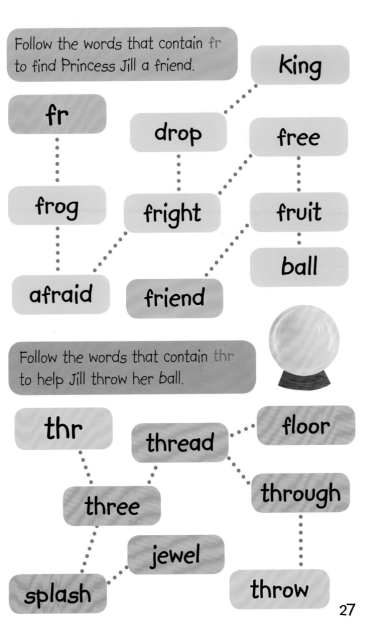

Follow the words that contain fr to find Princess Jill a friend.

king

fr

drop

free

frog

fright

fruit

ball

afraid

friend

Follow the words that contain thr to help Jill throw her ball.

thr

thread

floor

three

through

jewel

splash

throw

27

Rhyming words

Read and say the words in the flowers and point to other words that rhyme with them.

chip	this
Kiss	
hiss	bring

sing	you
King	
bring	bed

mean	dog
frog	
home	log

stick	**quick**	play
little		thick

snow	**throw**	go
me		live

give	**wish**	shiny
fish		dish

Now choose a word and make up a rhyming chant!

The **frog** and the **dog** are on a **log**!

Key words

Many common words can be difficult to sound out. Practice them by reading these sentences about the story. Now make more sentences using other key words from around the border.

Princess Jill loved **her** golden ball.

She dropped it in a river.

A frog said, "I'll get **your** ball."

Jill tricked the **little** frog.

not • your • asked • got • in

• said • little • a • her • had • made • day • she • we •

The frog came to Jill's **house**.

Jill felt annoyed **when** she saw the frog.

King Pip told **the** frog he could stay.

Jill kissed the frog **and** he turned into a prince!

The prince married Jill that **day**.

all · saw · and · when · house · the · called · people · my · about · up · you · they ·

old · there · like · into · of · with · was · dad

Picture dictionary

Look carefully at the pictures and the words.
Now cover the words, one at a time.
Can you remember how to write them?

ball

crown

frog

king

prince

princess

ring

river

windowsill